First published in 2005
by Hodder Children's Books

This edition published in 2015

Text and illustrations copyright © Mick Inkpen 2005

Hodder Children's Books
An imprint of
Hachette Children's Group
Part of Hodder & Stoughton
Carmelite House
50 Victoria Embankment
London EC4Y 0DZ

A catalogue record of this book is available from the British Library.

ISBN: 978 1 444 92410 7

10 9 8 7 6 5 4 3 2 1

Printed in China

An Hachette UK Company
www.hachette.co.uk

MIX
Paper from
responsible sources
FSC® C104740

Tickly Christmas Wibbly Pig!

Mick Inkpen

Hodder
Children's
Books

An imprint of Hachette Children's Group

Wibbly Pig has a
Christmas scarf,
made last year,
especially for him,
by Big Aunt Larlie.
So it is very special.

He doesn't like it
very much.

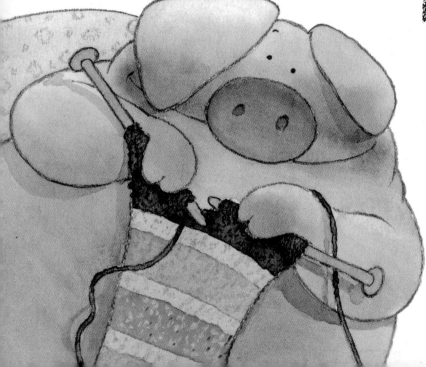

Wibbly has special gloves too. One of them arrived the Christmas before last.

And the other arrived the Christmas before that. Can you guess who made them?

Big Aunt Larlie.

The Christmas before
all of these Christmases,
Wibbly Pig was just
a little, baby piglet.
And he looked
like this.

And Big Aunt Larlie
was to blame.

Wibbly's special scarf
and gloves are tickly.

Itch!
Ooch!
Ouch!

But when it's cold outside,
and snow has fallen,
Wibbly Pig must wear his
special scarf, and his special
gloves. It's expected.

It is ten days before Christmas, and Wibbly Pig is helping to put up the Christmas decorations.

   This year, for the very first time, Big Aunt Larlie is coming to stay.

Big Aunt Larlie has bought herself some balls of wool – more balls of wool than usual.

Click! Clack! go her knitting needles.

Something very special is on the way.

Oh no.

Wibbly's friends do not have aunties like Big Aunt Larlie.

'I wonder what I will get this year,' says Wibbly Pig. 'I have tickly gloves. I have a tickly scarf.'

'I know!' says Spotty Pig. 'A tickly hat!'

It's Christmas Eve and
Wibbly Pig is investigating
Christmas parcels.
Itch! Ooch! Ouch!
The tree is tickly too!
Just like the hat he will
get from Big Aunt Larlie.

Ding! Dong! goes
the doorbell.
It's Big Aunt Larlie,
come to stay.

Wibbly Pig is
surprised.
'Aunt Larlie!' he says.
'You're wearing my
present!'

Big Aunt Larlie laughs.
'No I'm not, Wibbly
dear!' she says. 'This year
I've made a special
Christmas outfit for
myself!

This is YOUr present!'

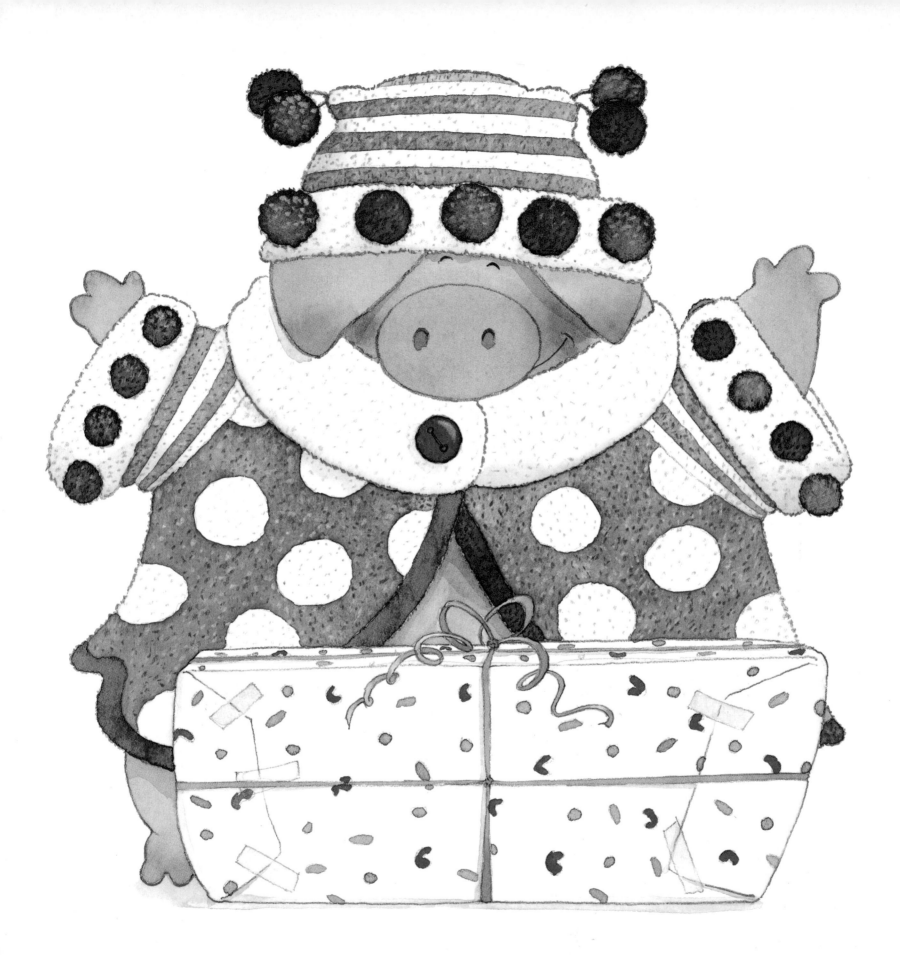

There is no tickly
hat for Wibbly Pig!
Oh dear!
What a shame!

This year
Wibbly Pig
will have to
make do with...

...whooosh!

A toboggan!

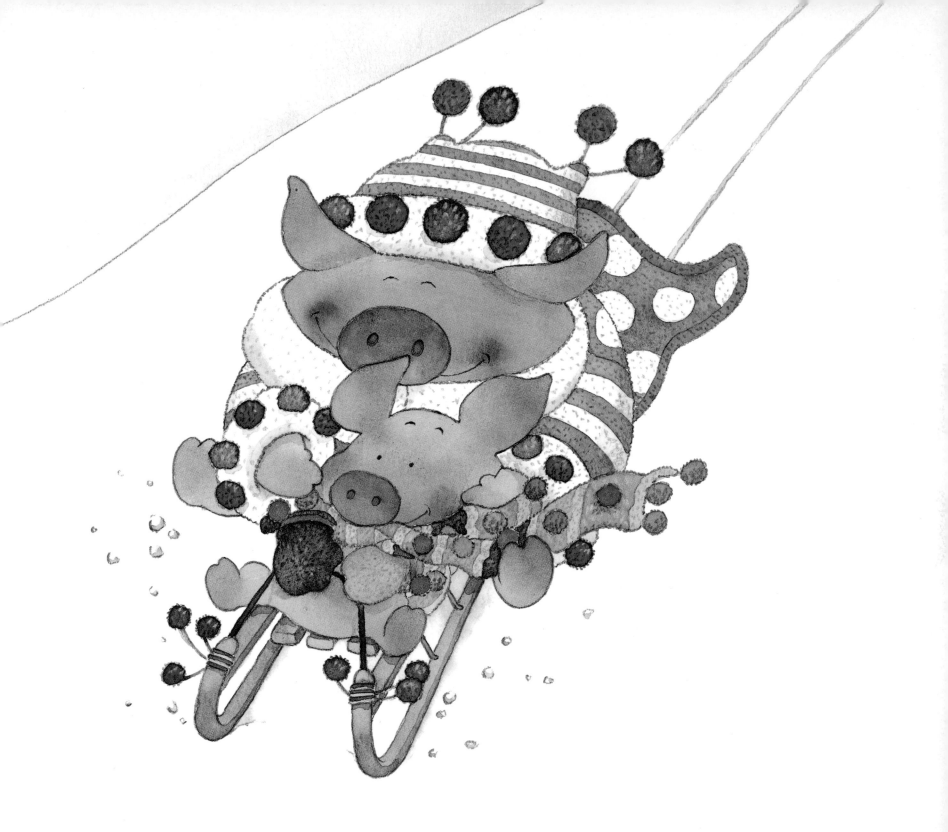

Happy Christmas, Wibbly Pig!

Great Kipper books
to share together

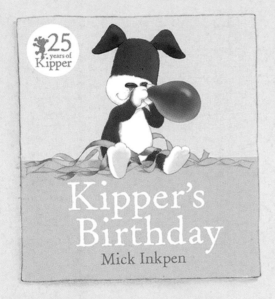

Kipper's
Birthday

Mick Inkpen

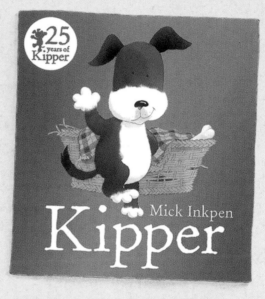

Mick Inkpen

Kipper

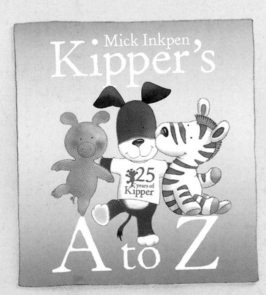

Mick Inkpen
Kipper's

A to Z

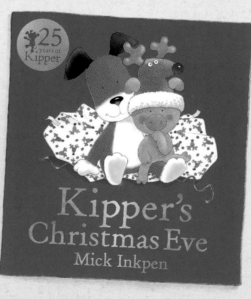

Kipper's
Christmas Eve

Mick Inkpen